W9-CFQ-637

Rocket Finds an Egg

Pictures based on the art by Tad Hills

Random House 🏠 New York

It is a sunny day!

Rocket and Bella play
in the meadow.

Rocket stops.

He finds an egg!

It is small, white,
and oval.

Rocket shows Bella.
"We have to find
its home!" Bella says.

Rocket and Bella
search the meadow.

They see Owl.

"Is this your egg?"

Rocket asks.

"No," Owl says.
"My eggs are
all here."

Rocket and Bella
find a bluebird.

The egg is not hers.

Her eggs are blue.

They ask
the little yellow bird.

The egg is too big
to be hers.

The friends ask
a bird with spots.

Her eggs

have spots.

They ask a red bird.

They ask a black bird.

They ask a brown bird.

They can not find
the egg's home!

Rocket and Bella
ask the chickens,
"Is this your egg?"

"No, it is not our egg,"
the chickens say.

At the pond,
the friends ask
the ducks.

The egg is not theirs.

"I am tired,"

Bella tells Rocket.

They take a break.

Then they hear

a <u>SPLASH!</u>

"My egg!"
a turtle says.
"That is my egg!"

"It is a turtle egg,"

Bella says.

"I looked for it
all day,"
the turtle tells them.

"We are glad
you found us!"
Rocket says.

Rocket and Bella
follow the turtle
to her nest.

ast,

the egg is home.